GO TO
WWW.MYGOGIRLSERIES.COM
FOR **FREE** GO GIRL! DOWNLOADS,
QUIZZES, READING CLUB GUIDES,
AND LOTS MORE GO GIRL! FUN.

Get to know the girls of

GO GIRL!

BY
CHRISSIE PERRY

ILLUSTRATIONS BY
ASH OSWALD

FEIWEL AND FRIENDS
New York

A FEIWEL AND FRIENDS BOOK
An Imprint of Holtzbrinck Publishers

Library of Congress Cataloging-in-Publication Data
Available

ISBN-13: 978-0-312-34652-2
ISBN-10: 0-312-34652-2

First published in Australia by E2, an imprint of Hardie
Grant Egmont. Illustration and design by
Ash Oswald.

First published in the United States by Feiwel and
Friends, an imprint of Holtzbrinck Publishers, LLC.

10 9 8 7 6 5 4 3 2

www.feiwelandfriends.com

CHAPTER ONE

Tamsin stepped over a pile of boxes to get into her new bedroom. She looked out the window to the backyard below. Trixie, her little black Scottie dog, was running around in circles and sniffing at the ground. Trixie seemed very happy with the move.

Tamsin wasn't so sure yet.

Part of her was excited. She was going to have a whole new life, and there would be a million things to discover in a new town. But mixed in with the feeling of excitement, there was a part of her that was just plain nervous.

Tamsin always felt shy with people until she got to know them. And when she started at school tomorrow, she wouldn't know anybody.

Tamsin heard her dad's footsteps, and then he was at the door.

"What do you think, honey?" he asked.

Tamsin shrugged. "It's a nice room, Dad," she said. "But it just doesn't feel like it's mine."

"You have to give it some time, Tamsin," he said, tapping a box. "When you've unpacked your clothes and toys, it will feel more like home."

"Yeah right, Dad," Tamsin laughed. "You're just trying to get me to do all the work!"

"Now, would I do such a thing?" her dad asked with a wink as he left the room.

Tamsin picked a box from the top of the stack and plopped it down on the carpet. Inside were all the posters and pictures from her old room.

Suddenly, she knew what would make her feel more at home. First, she put up a poster of Hilary Kim above her bed. Taylor Lind went up on the wall beside her.

Tamsin wasn't sure if these girls were friends in real life, but in her bedroom she liked to pretend that they always stuck together.

Tamsin looked through the box again.

She could hardly believe some of the pictures. There was even a giant-sized teddy bear poster. That would definitely, positively not be getting a space in her new room.

Tamsin had to sort through a lot of pictures that she had outgrown before she found the one she was looking for.

When she found it, she sat on the bed to study it. Her big brother, Julian, had made it for her. Julian had found a picture of Kayla Storm on the Internet, and had inserted a photo of Tamsin. It really looked as though Kayla had her arm around Tamsin, like they were best friends.

It was the coolest picture in the world!

Julian was a real whiz with computers.

Tamsin had begged him for ages to make the picture. She had to promise to clean his room for a month. She even picked up his toenail clippings off the floor. Gross factor? Ten out of ten! But it had been worth it.

Tamsin tried to stick the picture up on the wall. It took a few tries because the poster putty was pretty old.

She stepped back to take a look. It was starting to feel like her bedroom.

"Make sure you hang your uniform up," Dad called from downstairs. "You don't want it to be creased for tomorrow."

Tamsin opened another box and found the uniform on top of her regular clothes.

It would be weird to wear it tomorrow. At her old school, she just wore the school T-shirt with her favorite jeans and sneakers. Sometimes she would even call Karen, her best friend, and they would go to school in matching outfits.

In her new life, though, she was going to be wearing a blue shirt and a knee-length plaid skirt. And all the girls at school would have matching outfits!

Tamsin tried on the uniform and looked in the mirror. It was like a stranger was staring back at her. Just then, Trixie bounded into the room.

"Well, Trix, what do you think?" Tamsin asked.

Trixie made a whimpering sound, and stuck her nose under Tamsin's bed. Tamsin pulled her out.

"I know, I don't like it either," she said. "It's just not individual! But it's still me. Don't worry. At least, I'll blend in with the other girls at school tomorrow."

It's a new life for us, Trixie!

Trixie didn't seem so sure at first, but soon she was wagging her tail as usual. Tamsin crouched down to pet her. As she got up, her hand ran over a hidden pocket in the skirt.

"Look, Trix, a secret pocket!" she whispered.

Trixie gave a tiny bark, as though she was trying to whisper back in dog language.

"Dinner!" Dad called up the stairs.

Tamsin heard a whooshing sound as Julian slid down the banister, followed by a thud, as he jumped off the end.

Tamsin took off the skirt. Just as she was about to hang it in the closet, the picture of her and Kayla slipped off the wall. She

picked it up, folded it, and put it into her
secret pocket.

It would be nice to have it with her
tomorrow. It would be like a good luck
charm.

CHAPTER TWO

When they got to school, Tamsin's dad stayed with the other parents, while Tamsin wandered into a sea of uniforms. It was strange to listen to announcements outside on a basketball court. At her old school, Monday mornings always began with an assembly in the auditorium.

Tamsin sighed. She was going to have to get used to a lot of different things.

A group of boys stood out in front with a few teachers. One of the teachers lowered the microphone so a small boy could speak into it.

"On Saturday, we played football against the Malley Park Demons," he said. "We defeated them by ten points. Daniel Reisner got Most Valuable Player."

Everyone clapped. The boys sat down, and a group of girls walked up to the front. Tamsin thought they looked about her age. She wondered if they would be in her class.

One of the girls tapped on the microphone. Her brown hair was tied up into lots of little ponytails at different angles.

Tamsin felt a smile creeping onto her face. *Maybe you could still be an individual even if you did have to wear a uniform,* she thought.

The girls at this school look cool!

"Testing, one, two, three," said the girl. A few people laughed. "On Saturday, we played basketball against the Auburn Eagles," she said brightly. "We lost by twenty-three points, which is our best score so far!"

Everyone laughed loudly this time.

As the girl grinned and spun around, Tamsin started laughing, too.

"Thank you, Ivy," said the teacher, shaking his head. "Now, I would like you all to welcome a new student to this school. Tamsin Reilly will be in Mrs. Withers's

class. Tamsin, come up here please."

Tamsin looked down at her feet and made them walk to the front. Her face was burning with embarrassment as she stood in front of the whole school.

She didn't know what she was supposed to do, so she just waved. The students clapped and cheered.

So much for blending in, she thought.

CHAPTER THREE

After the assembly, a group of girls crowded around Tamsin.

"How come you've moved here?" asked one.

"You have nice hair, I like the curly parts. Is it natural?" asked another.

"It's cool you're in our class. Don't you think Mrs. Withers is the best?" asked a girl with dark braids.

Tamsin didn't know who to answer first. She felt a bit shy with everyone staring at her.

So many questions:

"My mom is a doctor, and we moved here because she got a new job," she started.

But before she could say anything else, Ivy, the girl with all the ponytails, pulled her towards the locker room.

"Look!" Ivy said. "We made you a name tag in art last week."

Ivy pointed to a peg. Above it was a tag with Tamsin's name and a drawing of a yellow daisy on it.

"Thank you," said Tamsin, grinning. "It's really pretty."

Tamsin felt good inside. It was nice of the girls to make her feel welcome.

Tamsin walked into class behind Ivy.

"I saved a seat for you next to me," Ivy said. "It used to be Casey's seat, but she got into trouble last week, and Mrs. Withers moved her over there."

Ivy pointed to another table where a girl with long red hair was pulling out her chair. Tamsin smiled at her. Casey shot back a strange look. It definitely *wasn't* a smile.

Casey banged her books hard on the table as she sat down. The sound made all

the kids look at her, but Ivy just kept on talking.

"Now, there's going to be a lot of names for you to remember," Ivy said kindly. She grabbed Tamsin's hand and pulled her over to the back of the room. "The best thing for you to do is to look at this photo chart when you forget who's who."

On the wall were labeled photos of everyone in the class.

"Thanks," Tamsin whispered. "I think I'll be looking at these a lot to begin with."

"You will have to bring one in, too," said a voice behind her. Tamsin turned around to see her new teacher.

When she had heard her name at the

assembly, Tamsin had expected Mrs. Withers to be a withering old lady. She wasn't like that at all. She was quite young for a teacher, and she had a bob hairdo and groovy square glasses.

"And Casey, don't forget that teachers have eyes in the back of their heads," Mrs. Withers said.

Tamsin looked over just in time to see Casey staring up at the ceiling. The other kids at her table were laughing.

Tamsin had a sinking feeling that Casey had been sticking her tongue out at her behind her back.

Tamsin was glad to start working. It made her stop wondering why Casey was being so mean. She wasn't so glad that their first subject was math. But after that, they did reading comprehension. The time went really quickly.

Before Tamsin knew it, the bell was ringing.

"Is it little lunch already?" Tamsin asked. All the kids at her table started to laugh.

"What's funny?" Tamsin asked.

"We call the the first break snacktime, or mini-recess," said Nina.

"But 'little lunch' is *so* cute!" said Ivy. "It makes me think of tiny little sandwiches."

Tamsin tried to smile. But suddenly, she missed her old school and her old friends. Everyone said "little lunch" there.

She wondered how many things were going to be different for her in this new school. Maybe she would have to learn a whole new language!

CHAPTER FOUR

"Hurry up with your food, or we won't have time to play jump rope," Ivy urged.

A little bit of half-chewed carrot shot out of Tamsin's mouth and onto Ivy's shirt as she giggled.

"Eew, gross!" Ivy exclaimed, laughing.

"I'm sorry," Tamsin said, picking off the carrot. "It's just that you sound exactly like my best friend, Karen. She was always telling me to hurry up with my food."

"Great minds think alike," said Ivy. "Karen must be smart. Does she like having your chewed-up carrot all over her top?"

"She prefers egg sandwiches," Tamsin said.

Both of them were laughing as Casey and Nina walked over to them. Casey was carrying a long jump rope.

"Hey guys, Tamsin can play jump rope with us, can't she?" Ivy asked.

Nina nodded, but Casey just shrugged.

"It's a free country," Casey said. "What's-her-face can twirl the rope."

"My name is Tamsin," Tamsin said, feeling hurt.

Casey just rolled her eyes, and handed

her the rope. Tamsin wasn't so sure that she wanted to play with Casey, but she did want to stick with Ivy, so she took the rope.

Tamsin hadn't played jump rope for ages. She concentrated to see how the game worked as Casey jumped in the middle.

The song went like this:

HIGH, LOW*
* DOLLY DOE
* SUGAR
SCISSORS*
* NORMAL
PEPPER!

If you landed on sugar, you had to go crazy, like you'd eaten too much sugar. For scissors, you had to do star jumps as you skipped. On normal, you could do anything you liked. But the most fun seemed to be when you landed on pepper. Then you had to jump double-time.

Casey landed on pepper.

As she jumped, her socks fell down over her ankles. Tamsin noticed that she was wearing an anklet. It was a pretty silver chain, with two little S's hanging off it.

Next, it was Nina's turn to jump. Tamsin almost stopped twirling the rope when she saw that Nina had the same anklet on.

When Ivy took her turn, Tamsin looked

closely at her ankles. Ivy had the same anklet on, too!

Finally, it was Tamsin's turn to skip. She wasn't very good. She couldn't seem to concentrate on the rhythm of the song.

Why do they all have anklets?

She was wondering why the three girls had matching anklets.

What did it mean?

She would definitely have to ask Ivy about it. Sometime when that Casey wasn't around.

CHAPTER FIVE

Tamsin took the phone into her bedroom and dialed Karen's number.

"TAMSIN," Karen shrieked. "I MISS YOU! HOW ARE YOU DOING? HOW'S MY FAVORITE DOGGY-DOO? HAVE YOU MADE SOME NEW FRIENDS?"

Tamsin held the phone away from her ear.

"Well, kind of," said Tamsin. "There's one girl here called Ivy. She reminds me a little bit of you. She's funny like you. And she lives on the same street as me."

"THAT'S LUCKY. YOU'LL BE

ABLE TO PLAY WITH HER ON WEEKENDS," Karen yelled.

"You don't have to yell, Kaz," laughed Tamsin. "I can hear you loud and clear."

Tamsin could hear Karen laugh through the phone line. It was the best sound she'd heard all week.

"OK, is this better?" Karen asked in a normal voice.

"Yes, much better," Tamsin giggled.

"So, are all the girls nice?" Karen asked.

Tamsin thought back over her first week of school. She had played with Ivy, Nina, and Casey every day. Ivy and Nina had both been really friendly.

But Casey seemed to be in a bad mood

all the time. She was always rolling her eyes at Tamsin, and she pretended she couldn't remember Tamsin's name.

Sometimes she was just as mean to Ivy and Nina without any reason.

"Ivy and Nina are both really nice," Tamsin tried to explain. "But I don't think Casey likes me very much. She's a bit mean, really. And there's something strange going on. The three of them all have the same anklet. It's got two S's hanging off it. They are my only friends here, but I feel like they have a secret, and I'm kind of left out."

Tamsin could hear crunching over the phone.

"Hang on," said Karen. "I need to think about this."

Tamsin smiled. Karen always ate potato chips when she needed to figure something out. She could nearly see Karen on the other end of the phone, crunching and thinking.

"I want to ask Ivy about it," said Tamsin, "but Casey is always around and I don't want to ask in front of her. She'll probably bite my head off!"

"It's a secret club!" Karen said. "That's what it is."

"So, what do you think SS stands for?" Tamsin asked.

"I don't know," said Karen. "But you *have* to find out. And you *have* to join. You could be missing out on all sorts of adventures!"

I think someone is at the door!

Trixie started barking and there was a knock on the door. Tamsin tried to ignore it, but Julian was on the computer, and he didn't hear anything when he was in computerland. Her mom and dad had gone shopping.

"Sorry, Kaz, I have to go," Tamsin said.

"OK, BUT FIND OUT WHAT'S GOING ON WITH THE ANKLET!" Karen yelled.

When Tamsin opened the door, she got a big surprise. It was Ivy, with a little sausage dog on a leash. Trixie was jumping all over the little dog.

"This is Rolf," said Ivy. "We were wondering if you would like to come for a walk with us."

"That would be great," Tamsin said.

She felt a grin creeping onto her face. Ivy was really lovely. And she had a dog. And she lived on the same street. Tamsin knew in her heart that they were going to be good friends.

As Tamsin clipped Trixie's leash onto her collar, she looked down. Ivy was wearing flip-flops. The anklet glinted in the sunshine.

The two S's looked a little bit like question marks. Tamsin was determined to get an answer.

CHAPTER SIX

"Rolf is adorable," Tamsin said, as they walked along. "Look, Trixie loves him."

Trixie kept trying to play with Rolf. She jumped on him, and then raced backward. After a while, Rolf got used to the game. He chased Trixie, and barked a little sausage dog bark.

"Trixie is very cute, too," Ivy said. "You know, I've wanted a dog *forever*. I still can't believe that Rolf is mine. He's the best friend ever!"

Tamsin grinned. "I know what you mean," she said. "I talk to Trixie all the time. Sometimes I think she understands me better than any human."

"Really?" Ivy asked. "That's what I do. I thought I was the only crazy one!"

"Well, you're not," Tamsin said. "I'm completely bananas."

She made a face to demonstrate how bananas she was. Ivy laughed out loud.

"You're funny, Tamsin," she said. "I'm glad you've come to our school. It's so cool to have another girl in our group."

The girls reached a park, and let the

dogs off their leashes. They were getting used to playing with each other now. They tumbled and rolled on the grass as the girls sat on the swings.

Tamsin took a deep breath. Finally, she had a chance to ask Ivy about the anklets.

"Why do you and Nina and Casey all have the same anklets?"

"I'm not supposed to tell," Ivy replied, biting her lip.

"Please, please, please," Tamsin begged. "It's killing me not knowing."

Tamsin put her hands up to her neck as though she was choking herself. Ivy laughed, and started to swing.

"Well, maybe if you *guessed* what they

were for, then it wouldn't really be telling," she suggested.

Tamsin started swinging a little, trying to keep in time with Ivy.

"You're in some kind of club?" she called on the way up.

Ivy nodded.

"And the other members of the club are Nina and Casey," Tamsin continued, going down.

Ivy nodded again.

"The club is called . . . Scary . . ."

This time Ivy shook her head. She stopped swinging. Tamsin scraped her feet on the ground so she would stop, too.

"It's called Secret Sisters," she whispered.

"Cool!" said Tamsin.

She understood right away why they'd called it that. She and Karen sometimes used to pretend they were sisters. It was fun.

"What do you do in the Secret Sisters Club?" she asked in a whisper. It was funny that they were both whispering, even though there was no one around to hear them, except for the dogs.

Tamsin guessed it was because of the "secret" part of the club's name. Secrets were always whispered.

"Oh, just stuff," said Ivy. "Casey has a clubhouse in her backyard. We meet there. Sometimes we try different makeup. Or we read magazines. Casey has tons of them. She loves looking at all the famous people. Other times, we just talk."

Suddenly, Tamsin felt really lonely. She

wished she had her own anklet, and was part of the group. She was getting used to her new school and new house, but it was still hard to be the new girl.

She thought of how she and Karen used to spend their Saturdays, reading magazines together and talking. Even though they didn't have a club, or anklets, they did have a fantastic friendship. Ivy seemed to read her mind.

"I've already asked if you can join, Tamsin," Ivy said softly.

"Really?" asked Tamsin, feeling a bit better already.

"Yep. We just need to have a vote, and we are going to do that on Monday. Everybody in the group has to agree. But I'm sure you'll get in."

Tamsin screwed up her nose. "What about Casey?" she asked. "I don't think she likes me that much."

Ivy looked shocked. "Of course Casey likes you," she said. "She's just had a lot of problems lately, and sometimes she gets upset and it makes her a bit . . . mean."

"What's wrong? What problems does she have?" Tamsin asked.

She wondered if Ivy was just trying to make her feel better about Casey.

"Casey might tell you herself when you join the Secret Sisters Club. We tell each other our secrets, because we know we can

trust our sisters. And on Monday, you will
be one of us!"

Tamsin nodded as she called Trixie. She
was glad that Ivy was trying to make her
part of the Secret Sisters Club. It sounded
really cool.

But in her heart, she wasn't so sure she
would get Casey's vote.

CHAPTER

SEVEN

On Monday, Tamsin was struggling with her art project when the bell rang for snacktime. They were making cards for Mother's Day.

Tamsin was trying to make a collage of her mom in her doctor's coat, but she hadn't finished. She wasn't sure how she was going to do her mom's curly hair.

"I've got some wool in the back," said

her art teacher. "If you want to stay in, I can help you."

"OK," said Tamsin. She wasn't absolutely sure that she wanted to miss out on snacktime. But she really wanted the card to be nice.

By the time Tamsin got outside, the girls were jumping rope.

"It's your turn," Ivy yelled.

Tamsin jumped into the rope, and started singing. She went through the whole song without tripping. When she sang it again, she landed on sugar.

She lets her arms and legs go all wobbly, and jumped like a complete nutcase. It felt good to be silly. Ivy and Nina laughed loudly. The more they laughed, the crazier Tamsin got.

Tamsin was laughing and jumping like a lunatic when she felt something slip from her skirt pocket.

Casey dropped the rope and picked up the piece of paper. As she unfolded it, Tamsin realized what it was. It was the picture of her and Kayla!

She had forgotten all about it.

"Look at this!" Casey yelled. "Wow, Tamsin knows Kayla Storm! Wicked!"

Tamsin felt as though her heart had stopped. She couldn't believe that Casey was finally paying some attention to her. And she also couldn't believe that the girls thought the picture was real.

Nina and Ivy looked over Casey's shoulder to get a better look.

"That is fantastic!" Nina said. "She's

even got her arm around you. Are you good friends or something?"

Tamsin didn't know what to say.

She knew she should tell them that Julian had made the picture. She knew she should tell them that she didn't really know Kayla.

What should I say?

But everybody was talking at once. And everybody was so excited.

"I don't really——" she began.

But Casey interrupted her. She looked very serious. "Well, Tamsin, you are the lucky new member of the Secret Sisters Club. We will have a special celebration tonight. Come to my clubhouse after school. And bring along that picture, so we can put it up on the wall!"

Tamsin didn't know what to say.

There were so many words swirling around in her head that it seemed impossible to pick the right ones.

Just then, the bell rang.

Casey stared at the picture again, and then handed it back to Tamsin.

As Tamsin looked at it, she felt Ivy's eyes scan the picture from behind her.

As she turned around, Ivy gave her a weird look. "Congratulations," she said softly.

CHAPTER EIGHT

"Tamsin, there is no magic fairy outside that window who is going to complete your work for you," said Mrs. Withers.

"Sorry," Tamsin mumbled.

She tried to concentrate on her schoolwork, but she just couldn't do it. She kept thinking about the Secret Sisters Club.

She couldn't wait! It would be so good

to be part of a club. She was sick of feeling lonely. But there was a problem. What if the girls had only accepted her because they thought she knew Kayla Storm?

She had never even met her! It didn't feel right.

Tamsin tried to focus on her worksheet, but her thoughts kept interrupting. She hadn't really *lied* about Kayla. But the girls thought the picture was real, and she hadn't told them it wasn't.

She didn't know what to do. If she told them the truth, maybe they wouldn't want her in the club. But if she didn't say anything, then she would be beginning new friendships with a lie.

Tamsin sighed. She remembered what Ivy had told her about how Casey liked looking through magazines with famous people in them. She looked around the classroom. Her eyes landed on the photos of all the kids in the class. She knew everyone's names now, so she didn't need the photos to remind her.

But suddenly, she had a brilliant idea.

At the end of the day, when everyone else had left the classroom, Tamsin took down the photos of Ivy, Nina, and Casey.

Then she headed home, with a job for Julian.

CHAPTER NINE

"Welcome to the Secret Sisters Club!" Casey said, opening the door of the clubhouse.

Tamsin gasped. It was the most amazing clubhouse she had ever seen. It was like a tiny house, with a real kitchen and bean-bag chairs spread all around.

Ivy and Nina were going through a big treasure chest that was filled with dress-up clothes.

"Hey, Tamsin," said Ivy. "What do you want to wear for the big ceremony?"

Tamsin chose a yellow gown and some dangly earrings.

"I feel like a princess," she said.

I'm Princess Tamsin.

All the girls laughed.

"Well, here's something that will make you feel even more like a princess," Nina said.

She held out an anklet, just like the ones the other girls wore.

"There's one for me?" gasped Tamsin. "Where did you get these?"

"My dad is a jeweller," Nina replied. "He made five of these especially for our club. Yours is the second-to-last one. Put it on."

Tamsin bit her lip. She wanted to be part of the club more than ever. But she didn't want it to be because of a lie.

"Wait a minute," she said. She put the anklet on a window ledge and reached into her bag.

"Cool, are you getting the photo of you and Kayla?" Casey asked. "Let's put it up on the wall, and then you can tell us how you know her. I can't wait to hear what she's like in real life."

Tamsin took a deep breath.

"I've never actually *met* Kayla," she said.

Casey and Nina looked confused. But Tamsin noticed that Ivy was smiling.

"Then how did you get that photo?" Casey asked.

"The same way I got *these* photos," Tamsin said. She pulled out three pictures, and handed one to each of the girls.

Nina took her photo, and sat on a beanbag. Ivy took hers over to the window. But Casey stood close to Tamsin, her eyes glued to her photo.

Then Tamsin waited.

It was as though time had stopped. It felt like her whole future rested on this moment. Every part of her body was tense. She felt the tip of the dress-up earring tapping against her neck, like the ticking of a clock.

Then suddenly, squeals and laughter rang out all over the clubhouse.

"Holy moly, it's me and Brianna!" Nina screamed. She jumped up from the beanbag, and danced around. "Love me, honey, all the time," she sang.

"What about me?" Ivy squealed. "Guess who I'm with in the photo?"

She lowered her head, and flicked her hair with her hands as she began to sing. "He had a cat, she had a dog, could they be any more ludicrous—"

"Ava!" Nina yelled. "Show me!"

Tamsin was still worried as she watched Nina and Ivy show their pictures to each other. Casey hadn't said a word. She just stared at the photo Tamsin had given her.

"Who are you with, Casey?" Ivy screamed.

Casey shut her eyes. Then she put her hands over her face. Tamsin's heart beat fast. She thought, *Casey is so angry, she can't talk.*

But suddenly, Casey started singing. "I don't want another silly crush. Don't want just anyone to hold—"

Casey's voice was amazing! Tamsin felt herself relax. Ivy and Nina joined in the song, and Tamsin joined in, too. Soon, all four of them were singing into cans of baked beans they got from a cabinet in the kitchen.

Yay! They loved the photos.

Finally, they all flopped onto the bean-bags, laughing.

Casey sat down on the same beanbag as Tamsin. "You are a rat, Tamsin Reilly!" she said. "You really had me fooled.

I thought you and Kayla must be friends. OK, Sisters, I think our new club member deserves the Secret Sisters Torture Chamber!"

Suddenly, all three girls started tickling Tamsin.

"I knew that picture was a fake," Ivy said as she tickled the bottom of Tamsin's feet. "Kayla's head is about twice the size of yours. That couldn't be right in true life, because your head is already huge!"

She held Tamsin down as the others tickled under her arms. Tamsin squealed. She could hardly get a breath between the giggles. It was fantastic!

Finally, they stopped tickling, and

Tamsin stopped giggling. Nina got the anklet off the window ledge.

All three girls helped to put it on.

Tamsin couldn't speak. She felt different with the anklet on. It wasn't just that she could feel it on her skin. It was like she could feel it in her heart. She didn't feel so new anymore, and she didn't feel so lonely. It was almost perfect.

There were just two things still worrying Tamsin. She took a deep breath. "Would you have let me join the Secret Sisters Club if you knew the photo wasn't real?" she asked Casey.

Casey looked puzzled.

"It's just that . . . well . . . you didn't

seem to like me so much *before* you saw the picture, and as soon as you saw it, you said I could be in the club. I guess I'm just wondering if you still want me to be a member, even if I don't know anyone famous and—"

"Man, you talk more than Ivy!" Casey interrupted. Then her face softened. "Tamsin, we had the vote while you were finishing that card for your mom. You were a Secret Sister *before* we even saw the picture."

Casey took a deep breath, and Tamsin noticed a tear in her eye. Ivy and Nina put their hands on Casey's shoulder.

"I'm sorry if I was a bit mean to you.

My mom and dad are splitting up," Casey whispered. "So, if I've been in a bad mood, that's why. I never used to get into trouble at school, either, but sometimes I just get so angry and frustrated, and then I do stupid things. It's really hard. . . ."

Tamsin felt like she was about to cry, too. That must be horrible for Casey. She touched Casey's shoulder along with Nina and Ivy. It felt like the four of them were linked. Not only by their anklets, but by their feelings.

"Have you told Mrs. Withers what's happening at home?" Tamsin whispered.

Casey shook her head.

"Well, I think you should. I think Mrs.

Withers would understand, and maybe she could help you."

Ivy and Nina nodded in agreement.

"OK," said Casey, picking up a magazine. "Now, would you girls get off my back so we can take the Kayla quiz? Tamsin should know all the answers, since Kayla is *such* a good friend."

Later, all the girls sat in a circle on the floor. They pretended they couldn't hear cars pulling up in the driveway. None of them wanted to go home.

"So, what do you think of our school,

and the Secret Sisters Club?" Nina asked Tamsin.

"I love the Secret Sisters Club," Tamsin replied. "And I *do* like school. It's just that—" Tamsin stopped talking.

She wasn't sure if she should tell them how much she missed Karen. Maybe her

Can I tell my NEW friends about my OLD friend?

new friends would feel strange if they knew about her old friend.

"What?" Ivy urged. Tamsin sighed.

"Well, I have this other friend named Karen. She is fantastic. She's good at everything. She can even surf, and I mean standing-on-a-real-long-board surfing! I think you guys would like her a lot. We've been friends since kindergarten. I really like it here, especially now that I'm a member of the Secret Sisters Club. But I really miss Karen. We e-mail, and we talk on the phone all the time. But it's not the same as seeing each other in real life."

The girls were quiet, but Tamsin could tell by their faces that they understood. It felt good to share her feelings with the Secret Sisters.

"Will Karen be able to come and visit you here?" Ivy asked.

Tamsin nodded. "Yep. She's coming in two weeks. But that still feels like a long time to wait."

"Tamsin, your mom is here," Casey's dad called.

Tamsin got up to leave, but the girls stopped her.

"We have to do the Secret Sisters good-bye," Casey said.

She put her hand in the center of the circle. Everyone else's hand went on top of it. When they pulled away, each girl touched her heart.

Tamsin knew what that meant. It was

like the girls were all connected now. Like they were there to take care of each other.

As Tamsin went down the steps of the clubhouse, Casey called out to her.

"Don't worry about Karen," she said.

CHAPTER TEN

Tamsin was super excited. It felt like *forever* since she'd seen Karen. There were so many questions to ask, and so many things to tell her.

Like how all the Secret Sisters had gone with Casey to tell Mrs. Withers about what was happening with Casey's parents.

Mrs. Withers had been so nice. She put Casey back on the same table as the others in class. Tamsin didn't mind at all that she had to move over a seat. It was just great that Casey seemed happier. And even when she *was* a bit mean, Tamsin understood.

Tamsin wished that she could take Karen to the Secret Sisters Club. They were having a Sunday meeting, but she knew she would have to miss it. The Secret Sisters Club had a few rules. One of the rules was that only members could go to meetings.

Tamsin waited outside on the front steps. She could hear the clicking of Julian's fingers on the keyboard of the computer.

"What time is it?" she called out.

"Five minutes later than the last time you asked!" Julian yelled back.

The time was dragging. There was still a whole hour to go before Karen was due.

Tamsin picked up a tennis ball and threw it for Trixie. It landed in a bush, and Trixie dived in after it. It was full of doggie slobber when she brought it back. Tamsin held it lightly between her fingers. She

Throw it again!
Throw it again!

threw it again. This time, it went out of the driveway. Trixie charged out behind it.

Trixie was taking a long time to bring the ball back. Tamsin heard her barking. Then she heard another dog bark. She raced up to the end of the driveway, and looked around the corner.

Ivy's sausage dog, Rolf, was rolling on the ground with Trixie. Both of them were too excited to get the ball.

It was like they had their own Secret Doggies Club!

Tamsin looked up to the end of the road. If Rolf was here, it should mean that Ivy was close behind. It took a while before she saw the girls. Ivy, Nina, and Casey were all walking up her street together. Tamsin waved, and walked towards them.

"Hey, Sisters," she said when she reached them. "What are you doing here?"

"We have something for you," said Ivy.

"Well, not really for *her*," Nina corrected.

"It *is* kind of for her," Casey argued.

Tamsin threw up her hands. "What are you fruit loops talking about?" she asked.

"This!" said Nina, holding up a Secret Sisters Club anklet. Tamsin noticed that all the girls were grinning.

"But I already *have* one," Tamsin said, confused.

"Isn't Karen coming to visit for the weekend?" Casey asked.

"Yes. She'll be here in an hour," Tamsin replied.

"Well, you can give her this," the girls all yelled together.

Tamsin sat on the curb. She felt a huge lump forming in her throat.

Can Karen be a Secret Sister?

"You mean that Karen can be a Secret Sister?" she asked.

All the girls nodded.

Tamsin lay back on the front lawn. She couldn't believe how good she felt. She almost wanted to cry out of happiness.

Just then, Rolf and Trixie jumped on top of her. Both dogs started licking her face. Tamsin felt the lump in her throat disappear as she sat up.

"Gross," said Casey. "I hope the new Secret Sister isn't the kind of girl who would let dogs lick her face!"

CHAPTER ELEVEN

There was too much happening at Casey's house to have the Secret Sisters meeting in her clubhouse. Tamsin was kind of glad.

The clubhouse was great, but she was beginning to love her bedroom, too. Her parents had let her choose her own curtains and duvet cover, and the whole wall was covered with her favorite pictures.

It was exciting to have all of her best friends in there.

Karen closed the door. "I absolutely love this anklet!" she said. "Thanks for letting me be a Secret Sister."

Casey smiled. "Well, you're not actually a real Secret Sister until you take the Kayla quiz," she said, pulling out a tattered magazine.

"You must carry that thing with you all the time," Ivy teased.

Casey gave her one of her evil looks.

"OK, OK," Ivy laughed. "What star sign is Kayla Storm?"

Karen raised her eyebrows. "Um, is she Scorpio?" she said.

The Secret Sisters are fantastic!

"Correct," Ivy yelled. "Now, I think we need to get a photo of the Secret Sisters. Where's your brother, Tamsin?"

"Just follow the clicking noises," Tamsin said.

The girls danced their way into the

living room, and started talking to the back of Julian's head as he typed away on the computer.

"Hello, Tamsin's brother," Casey said.

Julian turned his head. "Hmpff," he said.

"We were just wondering if you'd take a photo of us, and make it into one of those cool posters you do."

Julian stopped typing and stared at them. "Hmm," he said. "I guess I can do that . . . if you go to the store and get me some candy."

"OK," Ivy said.

"And wash Dad's car, clean the hamster cage, and pick up Trixie's poo."

The girls looked at each other, and burst out laughing.

"All right!" Casey screamed. "We'll do all your disgusting jobs."

Julian got out his digital camera.

The girls lay on top of each other on the couch. They were all grinning, and they all had their legs up to show off their anklets. The flash went off, and they looked at the picture.

Tamsin felt her heart swell. It was the best day of her life. She had all her friends together. Her new life was starting to feel even better than her old one.

The Secret Sisters Club was the best!

Julian plugged the camera into the computer.

"So, which famous person do you want me to paste in with you ding-dongs?" he asked.

The Secret Sisters looked at each other. They all had the same idea.

"We don't want anyone else in the photo," Tamsin said. "We like it just the way it is."

GO GIRL!

If you loved reading about Tamsin, you shou meet the other GO GIRL! girls.

LUNCHTIME RULES
BY VICKI STEGGALL

✳ **Ant**

THE WORST GYMNAST
BY THALIA KALKIPSAKIS

✳ **Gemma**

SISTER SPIRIT
BY THALIA KALKIPSAKIS

✂ **Cassie**

GoGIRL! #2

THE WORST GYMNAST

BY
THALIA KALKIPSAKIS

Gemma stood at the start of the runway, ready to run. She pictured a handspring in her mind—*legs together, butt tucked in . . . up and over the vault.* But she didn't run yet. She was waiting for Michael to nod his head.

Michael was Gemma's gymnastics coach. He kicked a safety mat into place, then stood next to the vault, ready to help Gemma over.

Finally, Michael nodded his head.

Gemma wiped her hands on her legs and looked at the vault. Then she ran.

She ran fast, pumping her arms.

As Gemma ran up to the vault, Michael reached in to help her over.

But as Gemma jumped, her foot slipped. Her legs flew apart and her butt stuck out. She did it all wrong. She was just about to crash into the vault when Michael pushed her up and over—*legs apart, butt out, almost over* . . .

Thud!

One of Gemma's legs—out of control —hit Michael in the face. Gemma landed on her back, with her arms and legs out.

It had been a very bad vault.

Gemma lay on her back, surprised that she had made it over. That had been close. Was anything hurt? Nothing.

Then Gemma remembered the thud. She rolled off the mat.

Michael stood in the same spot with his face in his hands.

"Sorry," Gemma said quietly.

This was bad. Was Michael alright?

"I'm so sorry," Gemma said a bit louder.

Michael lifted his head.

Blood trickled from his nose onto the palm of his hand.

"Are you alright?" Gemma asked, but it felt like a silly question. His nose was bleeding.

Michael looked at Gemma and shook his head. He wiped his nose with a tissue. "Team meeting," he said, and walked away.